Daveney,
The Everyday Princess

By Kimberly N. Washington
Illustrated By TullipStudio

Printed in the United States of America
ISBN 9781736264904

To my daughter Daveney, thank you for inspiring me to leave fear behind and embrace possibility. I love you!

Daveney's Divine Beginning

One night in January 2013 I had a dream. The name Daveney Nicole was written on a chalk board. I got up and prayed for this Daveney Nicole, then went back to sleep and had the same dream again in the same night. Once again, I got up and prayed for this Daveney Nicole person. I did a Google search for the name "Daveney Nicole" and no one was listed with this name combination. I wrote the dream down in my journal. I went back to sleep and the next morning I shared the dreams with my husband, Robert. We discussed it and to be honest we somewhat forgot about the dream.

On the morning of March 19, 2013 (Robert's birthday), I wasn't feeling well. I decided to take a home pregnancy test and learned that I was pregnant. I woke my husband up at about 2:21 am and asked him to tell me what he saw on my test because the second line was faint. It took him several times to see the second line because I woke him up out of some GOOD sleep (lol). Once he recognized the second line, he asked what it meant. I told him I was pregnant, and he began to cry and pray immediately laying hands on my stomach and praying for the baby and myself.

My husband and I desired a boy (first) and we activated our faith and prepared the nursery for a boy, purchased boy clothes, made sure everything was in line for our son. Fast forward... we went to the sonogram appointment to find out the health and to confirm the sex of the baby because we knew it was going to be a boy. The sonographer asked if we wanted to know the sex, and of course my husband was like, sure but we know it's a boy. She said, "Well I see 3 lines." We both told her to look again. Of course, my husband did not know what "3 lines" meant. So, she finally told us it's a girl and we were heartbroken because we had done everything we knew. We did not understand why it didn't work... because our faith had worked for us every time in the past that we activated it.

On our way home, we began to talk to God about our disappointment. God immediately brought the two dreams back to our remembrance that I had in January. The name He had written on the chalkboard, "Daveney Nicole" is a girl's name. But because we did not seek the Lord on what the dreams meant, we somewhat forgot about them and did not know they were prophetic. The last thing God said to us about this experience that we carry with us every day is, "Your faith can not work outside My will." Then it all clicked. The two dreams in January represented two months later (March) I would be pregnant with Daveney Nicole Washington.

We are a testament of God's sovereignty. He knows best and we would not trade her for any boy! She has been the GREATEST blessing to us and is the inspiration for this series. I'm sure you will enjoy seeing life through the eyes of our Everyday Princess, Daveney.

Hi, I'm Daveney!
I'm seven years old.

I love to play dress up. My favorite costumes are princess dresses.

One day, I asked my Mommy to take me to the toy store to buy a Black princess doll.

We didn't see a single one. We left without buying anything.

Mommy and Daddy sat down to talk with me because I was sad.
I didn't understand why finding a Black princess doll was so hard.

We saw a lot of white
princess dolls in the store.

"Why aren't there any Black princess toys and books? Is it because there aren't any in real life?" I asked.

Mommy said, "There are Black Kings, Queens, Princes, and Princesses." She showed me pictures of African royalty on the computer.

"Then why didn't we find any at the store?" I asked Mommy. Mommy answered, "It is not easy to explain. There is no good reason.

Some people do not think it is important to have products for Black people. So they don't make things for us to buy."

"This is why we do our best to buy Black things from Black people. That helps them put more Black items in the stores."

"When you're a little older, I'll tell you more about how these things got to the way they are now," Mommy promised.

"Daveney, did you know that you're a princess?" Daddy asked me. "No, I'm not," I mumbled. Daddy said, "You are too."

He told me that anyone who follows God is royalty. He said because I am God's child, I am a princess!

"But I don't have a palace or anything special like the princesses I watch in the movies," I complained.

"You have a lot of special talents and skills, Daveney," Mommy replied.

"You're very kind, energetic, and the BEST helper!

You can use all these things to make the world a better place, and help other Black kids find toys that look like them."

After dinner, I asked Mommy if I could do a craft. Mommy said yes. I went and got my supplies and went to work.

"What are you going to make?" Mommy asked me. "It's a surprise. You'll see," I said.

I worked in my room for a while. When I finished my craft, I started playing with my dolls.

When Mommy came upstairs to check on me, four of my dolls had crowns on their heads.

"Mommy, I made crowns for my dolls so they could be princesses. I told them what you and Daddy said about being princesses."
Do you think I can make more crowns and give them to my friends so they can make their dolls princesses too?"

"That's a good idea, Daveney!" Mommy exclaimed. "Let's see how we can make that happen." I was so happy that I could help my friends make their dolls princesses too.

That night when I said my prayers, I thanked God for making me a princess and making me special so I could help other little kids.

"Thank you, Mommy and Daddy for cheering me up!
I'm happy I'm a princess...everyday!"

Yes, you are a princess every day, whether you wear your costume or not. God made you special and you get to show that wherever you go," Mommy told me. "You don't need a crown, wand, or a special dress. You're who God made you to be!"

"But I can wear my dress and crown, can't I?" I asked Mommy. "Of course!" Mommy answered, laughing.

"Good night Queen Mommy and King Daddy," I said.

"Good night Princess Daveney," Mommy and Daddy said.

About the Author

Kimberly N. Washington is married to Robert, and they have one child, Daveney. My life's passion is empowering girls and women of all ages to embrace their God-given identities. To that end, I founded a faith-based women's empowerment initiative called mpowHer! This book, the first in a forthcoming series, furthers my mission by focusing on encouraging young girls to maximize their potential. I am excited to add children's book author to my list of accomplishments!

9 781736 264904